D1489411

THE
MIDNIGHT
CASTLE

THE MIDNIGHT CASTLE

CONSUELO JOERNS

Lothrop, Lee & Shepard Books
New York

Library of Congress Cataloging in Publication Data
Joerns, Consuelo. The midnight castle. Summary: A family of mice makes itself at home in a toy castle
only to find that the castle and its medieval inhabitants become real at the stroke of midnight.
[1. Mice—Fiction. 2. Space and time—Fiction. 3. Knights and knighthood—Fiction] I. Title.
PZ7.J59Mi 1983 [Fic] 82-24923 ISBN 0-688-02090-9 ISBN 0-688-02091-7 (lib. bdg.)

For

PC

&

NK

*M*aggie was stuffing hay into the cracks of the ramshackle house to keep out the wind. Pebble, Pocket and Thimble were helping, and even tiny Pouf hauled hay in his wagon. Boswell was about to go out again with his sack. He was busy gathering seeds for the winter.

"Take Pouf with you," said Maggie. "We're off to get more hay, and you know how Pouf always gets lost in the meadow!"

Boswell hoisted Pouf up on his back. "Hang on tight," he said, "we're going on a great adventure." Boswell knew there were some seeds on the high windowsill of an old house. With Pouf on his back, he went over a nearby hill, up a tree, down a branch, and jumped onto the sill. The seeds trailed through a broken windowpane. Boswell peeked inside and saw a dark, gloomy playroom. There were some old toys on the dusty floor, and a grandfather clock covered with cobwebs. The seeds zigzagged across the floor and disappeared into a castle!

Boswell's heart thumped. He stared at the castle. It had stone towers with banners flying from the battlements. There was a deep moat around it and a drawbridge that was down, making a bridge over the moat. He pulled Pouf through the broken pane and then ran for the drawbridge. He was so eager to explore the castle, he forgot to take Pouf with him.

Two knights with crossed spears guarded the entrance on the drawbridge. They were very flat and made of tin. Boswell toppled them into the moat. His sack fell in too, by mistake, so he had to leave it. The moat was dry but very deep.

Inside, the Great Hall was splendid. Banners hung from high rafters. There were glorious tapestries on the walls, and shields and lances. Boswell was frightened by dogs in front of the fireplace and almost ran, but they turned out to be tin. One little push and they fell flat. He stepped over them and followed the trail of seeds through a passageway.

It led to the kitchen where he found a big, plump sack of seeds, much too big to carry. Boswell was so excited, he raced out of the kitchen (knocking down some tin cooks on the way), through the Great Hall, over the drawbridge, across the play-room floor, out the broken pane, along the branch, down the tree, over the hill, and all the way home. He could not wait to tell Maggie!

"Where is Pouf?" demanded Maggie. Boswell had been try-ing to tell her about the castle. "I don't care about the castle! I want my Pouf!" Boswell couldn't believe he had left Pouf behind. He was sick with worry as he backtracked and led the whole family through the broken windowpane.

"There he is!" cried Thimble. Pouf was sitting on a toy lion near the moat. When they pulled him off he shouted "No!" and kept on shouting "No!" as they dragged him into the castle. Maggie hugged Pouf and dried his tears, but he still wanted the lion.

With Pouf safe, Maggie wanted to see the castle. Pebble, Pocket and Thimble ran all over, and were soon at the top, looking out from the battlements. When Boswell took Maggie to see the big sack of seeds, they tripped over the cooks in the kitchen. This made Maggie so nervous that Boswell threw them into the dungeon and bolted the door.

It was getting dark and they were all hungry. Boswell lit the torches in the Great Hall. Maggie set about making a feast. They lit the logs in the fireplace too, to warm up the castle. Then they took tapers and all found beds to sleep in for the night. There was plenty of room in one of the towers for Pebble, Pocket, Thimble and Pouf. They bounced on the feather beds and threw pillows at one another. Pouf was knocked down, so Boswell picked him up and carried him.

Boswell and Maggie climbed to the other tower where they found a lovely room. There was a canopied bed with curtains drawn around it. When Maggie drew them back, they saw a tin figure wearing a crown, lying on the bed. Pouf gazed at her in wonder. "She's not real, Pouf," said Boswell. "She's in our bed," said Maggie. "Out she goes!" said Boswell.

She was so flat she could easily slide through the narrow castle window. They picked her up. "No!" screamed Pouf as he grabbed her hand, but it slipped through his paw when she fell out the window. A ring came off in his paw. Pouf did not dare look at it because Maggie was giving him a little shove. "To bed, to bed, it's very late. Hurry up, Pouf." And off he went with Maggie, to be tucked into bed with the others.

Inside the castle, the torches were burning low. It was dark and spooky *outside* the castle too, so Boswell went down and pulled up the drawbridge. Now all was quiet. Snug at last in the canopied bed, he fell asleep before Maggie came back.

THE QUEEN'S RING

Pouf was wide awake. *Something was happening!* Behind the castle, the grandfather clock began to toll the twelve strokes of midnight so loudly that the castle trembled. For Pouf, it seemed like forever between each *bong*, yet everything else was happening so fast! Bright moonlight streamed through his window. He felt the ring in his paw grow heavy.

Pouf jumped out of bed and looked at it in the moonlight. It was solid gold and shaped like a dragon, with spiny ridges along its back and folded wings.

Pouf leaned out the window to try to see the lady with the crown, below. He saw the moat gleaming in the moonlight. The moat was filled with water! Now he saw that there were no walls to the playroom outside the castle, and no ceiling. What had been a wooden floor was rolling countryside with hills and forests. Stars twinkled in the night sky.

There was a sudden, deafening roar of a lion. Pebble, Pocket and Thimble woke up and ran around the room, squeaking. In the other tower, Boswell and Maggie sprang out of bed, clutching each other in fear.

Pouf hung out of his window trying to find the lion. A horn sounded far away. Then he heard running feet below and voices shouting, "The King! The King has come back! Wake up the Queen!" There was a clattering of horses' hooves.

Out of the darkness, a procession of knights rode forth carrying banners. They were led by a magnificent horseman wearing

a crown. From the shadows a crowd gathered. Drums thudded. Trumpets blared. Acrobats tumbled. A bear danced.

"Bring torches!" shouted a voice. "The King comes! Lower the drawbridge! Wake up the Queen!" Soon torches were blazing everywhere. Some yelled, "The castle guards are drowned!" A murmur of disbelief went through the crowd. There was a clanging of metal as the knights drew their swords. "Lower the drawbridge," they shouted, "in the name of the King!"

As the knights came near, another cry went up, a most terrible one: "The Queen is in the moat! Save the Queen!" There was an awful silence while the tin Queen was fished out of the moat. Then the King was heard sobbing, "Who has done this dreadful deed?" By now, Boswell and Maggie were leaning out their tower window, and Pebble, Pocket and Thimble were up on the battlements looking down. They all heard Pouf's small voice below say, "She was thrown out the window."

Boswell and Maggie jumped back into the canopied bed and pulled the curtain all around. Their hearts were pounding wildly. They felt all eyes looking up to their window, the Queen's bedroom. *They* had killed the Queen! But she had not even seemed real. The confusion and noise outside were awful.

The King had the Queen in his arms and was riding around in a distracted sort of way. The knights were preparing to attack the castle. They were leaning a ladder against the tower. Now they climbed right up and over the battlements and captured Pebble, Pocket and Thimble.

Then they hauled Boswell and Maggie out of bed and threw them all in the dungeon. When they did this, the cook and his kitchen helpers swarmed out, happy to be free. The knights lowered the drawbridge, and the King rode in.

So far, no one had seen Pouf. He was on his way to the tower where he thought Boswell and Maggie were. But when he got there he did not find them.

Instead, he found the King. He had laid the tin Queen on her bed and was gazing at her tenderly, as if in a dream. Pouf, too, stared at the Queen. Suddenly the King shouted, "The ring! The Queen's ring is gone! She is doomed if the ring isn't found. Search the prisoners. Find the ring!" The King's voice cracked with grief and tears ran down his face.

Pouf held out his paw to the King. On it lay the ring. The King was startled. He grabbed Pouf's paw and almost crushed it in his grip, yet his voice was full of hope. "You took the ring, so it is *you* who must slay the dragon to bring back the Queen." But the King's hopes soon sank. "How tiny you are! Have you ever fought a dragon?" Pouf did not dare tell the king he had never fought even a mouse.

"Listen carefully, Fur Creature," said the King. "The dragon fire will melt all weapons. You must slay the dragon with your paws, and give the ring back to the Queen." Just then the grandfather clock struck its terrible *bong* that shook everything to the roots.

"The eleventh stroke of midnight! So little time!" cried the King, and he dragged Pouf down the tower steps in great leaps. "Quick! Before the twelfth toll! If anything gives you courage, call upon it NOW!"

POUF FIGHTS THE DRAGON

Suddenly they were outside the castle. The King placed the ring on a rock and, lifting his sword, he struck it with all his force. There was a flash as the ring exploded into a monster dragon, spitting fire. Smoke was everywhere. Pouf heard the lion roar, and then he remembered what the King had said and wished he had the courage of a lion.

Pouf had been thinking of the toy lion, so when a *real* lion bounded up roaring, he was frozen with fear. He stood between the dragon and the lion, unable to move.

But now the lion nudged him so gently, and his mane was so soft and inviting, that Pouf climbed onto his back. From the castle battlements, the knights saw and cheered.

The dragon lashed its tail at Pouf, then twisted and lunged at him. Flames poured from its open jaws. Pouf dodged the sharp claws and fangs. His fur was scorched and he choked on dragon smoke. The lion let out a roar like thunder, but Pouf could feel him shake with fear.

Suddenly a giant ball of fire flew out of the dragon, aimed right at the lion, too fast to escape. Pouf's paw shot up to shield the lion and he shouted "NO!" at the top of his lungs. Instantly, the fireball sputtered out and the clock struck the last toll of midnight. The dragon sizzled, shrinking smaller and smaller, until with a *clink*, it became a ring again.

Pouf felt the lion stiffen beneath him and he climbed off. The playroom floor was wood again. The King was turning to tin! The sound of the *bong* was fading.

Pouf ran up to the tower and slipped the gold ring onto the finger of the Queen. Had he saved the Queen or hadn't he? He didn't know. He knew only that everything had changed and he wanted his family.

He ran through the castle, hollering. The torches had gone out, and it was very dark. Shouts came from the dungeon. He could barely reach the bolt to unlock the door. Pebble, Pocket, Thimble, Boswell and Maggie burst out, covered with spider webs and almost crazy from the awful things they had seen in the dungeon.

Boswell and Maggie herded everybody out of the castle. They longed to be safe and cozy in the ramshackle house, in their own beds with the patched-up quilts. Pouf did not want to go. There was too much he did not understand. He grabbed Boswell's jacket, pulled him back and cried, "Is the dragon really dead? Will the ring save the Queen?"

"What dragon? What ring? You're dreaming, Pouf!" said Boswell. "We've all been scared out of our wits in the dungeon and now we're going home *before anything else terrible happens!*"

On the long trek home Pouf dragged behind, stumbling. Finally he had to be carried, and was asleep when Maggie laid him on his bed. She gently cleaned his scorched fur, which still smelled of dragon smoke. He dozed all through the next day and went soundly to sleep that night as well.

BONG! Pouf woke up. Was he dreaming or was something happening again? He thought he heard, ever so faintly, a clock begin to strike midnight. The rumble of horses' hooves came closer. The noise seemed loud but no one else woke up. Suddenly the Queen was at the foot of his bed, smiling and reaching for his paw. The lion was there too, nuzzling him.

A trumpet blared and the King appeared. "Kneel," said the King. Pouf knelt. "I knight thee Sir Pouf Lion Heart," said the King as he touched Pouf's shoulders with the blade of his sword. The knights outside gave a mighty cheer. Quickly, the King took the Queen's hand and they left at once. Outside, Pouf heard the King shout, "Make haste!" and the whole troupe galloped off, the lion bounding beside them. Pouf watched until he could see them no longer. Far away he heard the clock toll the last stroke of midnight.

The next morning Maggie coaxed Pouf awake. He tried to tell her what had happened. "A dream?" said Maggie, hugging him. Shouts came from Boswell. He was dragging a plump sack through the door. "Look!" he said, "seeds from the castle! And a roll of tapestries outside. How did they get here? Come help me, Pouf. I begin to think this has something to do with *you!*"

They hung the tapestries on the walls, and all agreed they were better than hay to keep out the wind. There was a very small one that Pouf got to put on his bed as a cover.

Boswell refused ever to go back to the castle (maybe because he was so frightened of the dungeon), but Pouf *knew* that somehow he would see the lion again, and the King and Queen, perhaps some night when he least expected to.

THE END